DISNEY · PIXAR
Cars

Adventure Story

PaRragon

Bath · New York · Singapore · Hong Kong · Cologne · Delhi
Melbourne · Amsterdam · Johannesburg · Auckland · Shenzhen

First published by Parragon in 2011
Parragon
Queen Street House
4 Queen Street
Bath BA1 1HE, UK

Lightning McQueen is fast, but sometimes it takes more than just speed to win a race. To find out if Lightning McQueen has what it takes to become a real champion, buckle your seat belt and turn the page to begin the ride!

It was the final race of the season and Lightning McQueen was in the lead. It looked like he was about to become the first rookie to ever win the Piston Cup. There was just one problem – he wouldn't listen to his pit crew. "We need tyres now! Come on!"

Lightning yelled, "No, no, no, no – no tyres, just gas!" Then he roared back onto the track. "Chequered flag here I come."

But he *should* have listened because on the final turn his rear tyres blew out. As Lightning desperately lunged for the finish line, his two main competitors, The King and Chick Hicks, caught up with him. It was a photo finish and a three-way tie!

It was decided that a tiebreaker race would be held in California in one week. So, Lightning climbed into his trailer and set off with his driver, Mack. "California here we come!"

Later, after many hours of driving, a weary Mack started to pull off the road. "Just stoppin' off for a quick breather, kid. Ol' Mack needs a rest."

But Lightning wanted to be the first one to California. "Absolutely not! We're driving straight through all night 'til we get to California. We agreed to it."

Poor Mack kept driving while Lightning went to sleep in the trailer. Mack tried to stay awake, but he was exhausted. As he started to doze off, some road pranksters began tossing him back and forth across the lanes. In the jostling, the trailer door accidentally opened. When one of the pranksters sneezed, Mack was startled awake, causing Lightning to slip off the ramp of the trailer and into the middle of the oncoming traffic!

Jolted awake, Lightning looked everywhere for his driver. "Mack! Mack! Mack, wait for me!" He followed a truck off the Interstate, but it wasn't Mack.

Confused and lost, Lightning had just zoomed past a sign that read "Radiator Springs" when a police cruiser turned on its siren. "Oh, no."

As Lightning slowed down, Sheriff's car backfired. Lightning mistook the sound. "He's shooting at me! Why's he shooting at me?"

Terrified, he zoomed into the little town of Radiator Springs where he lost control and crashed into just about everything. He even got tangled with the town statue and dragged it down the road. When it was all over, Lightning was dangling upside down, caught in telephone wires and the road was ruined. Sheriff glared at him. "Boy, you're in a heap of trouble."

The next morning, Lightning awoke to find himself being greeted by a rusty old tow truck. "Morning, Sleepin' Beauty!"

"Ahhhh! Take whatever you want, just don't hurt me!" Lightning tried to race away, but he couldn't move. The town had put a parking boot on his tyre.

The tow truck smiled. "You're funny, I like you already! My name's Mater."

"Mater?"

"Yeah, like tuh-mater but without the 'tuh'."

Just then Sheriff rolled up. "What did I tell you about talking to the accused?"

"To not to."

"Well, quit your yappin' and tow this delinquent road hazard to Traffic Court."

The next thing Lightning knew, he was in a courtroom filled with angry townsfolk. Sheriff spoke.

"Anyone wanna be his lawyer?"

Mater volunteered. "I'll do it Sheriff."

Just then the doors burst open. "All rise, the honourable Doc Hudson presiding!"

An official-looking car named Doc rolled onto a lift and was raised to the top of the judge's podium. "Alright, I wanna know who's responsible for wrecking my town, Sheriff. I want his hood on a platter."

But for some strange reason, after Doc took one look at Lightning, he stopped short. "Throw him outta here, Sheriff. Case dismissed!"

Lightning couldn't believe his good luck. Then a beautiful Porsche, entered. "Sorry I'm late, Your Honour."

Thinking she was from his lawyer's office, Lightning interrupted. "Hey, thanks for coming, but we're all set. He's letting me go."

But Sally wasn't from Lightning's lawyer's office, she was the town attorney. Lightning was stunned when she begged Doc to reconsider. "Come on, make this guy fix the road. The town needs this."

Sally told the court that if it wasn't fixed the town wouldn't survive and since Lightning was the one that did the damage he should be the one responsible for fixing it. "So what do you want him to do?"

"FIX THE ROAD!!" Reluctantly, Doc changed his mind. So, Lightning was sentenced to remain in Radiator Springs and fix the road.

Later that day, Doc introduced Lightning to Bessie, a road-paving machine. "So we're gonna hitch you up to sweet Bessie, and you're gonna pull her nice."

"Whoa. Whoa, whoa! How long is this gonna take?"

"Well, a fella does it right, it should take him about five days."

When Lightning heard this he knew he'd never make his race. As soon as Mater removed his parking boot, he zoomed away, leaving them in a cloud of dust. "Woo-hoo! Goodbye, Radiator Springs!" But just then Lightning's engine began to splutter. "No, no, no, no. Outta gas? How can I be outta gas?"

Sheriff and Sally caught up with him. "Boy, we ain't as dumb as you think we are."

"H-h-how did you...?"

"We siphoned your gas while you were passed out. Ka-chow."

It didn't take Lightning long to realize that the sooner he finished repairing the road, the sooner he was going to make it to California. So, he quickly set to work and within an hour had finished the job. "Just say thank you, and I'll be on my way."

But as the townsfolk looked at the road all they saw was a bumpy mess of splattered tar. "It looks awful!"

"Look, Doc said when I finished, I could go. That was the deal."

Doc pulled up. "The deal was you fix the road, not make it worse. Now scrape it off."

"Hey, look grandpa, I'm not a bulldozer, I'm a race car."

"Oh, ho, ho. Is that right? Then why don't we just have a little race? Me and you. If you win, you go and I fix the road. If I win, you do the road my way."

Lightning happily accepted Doc's challenge. He felt there was no way he could lose.

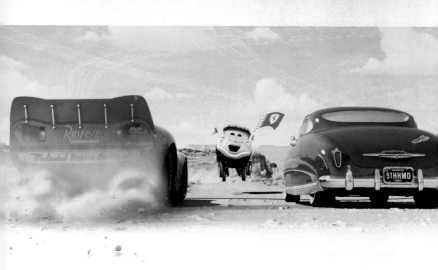

Later, at a dirt track outside of town, the two cars sat at the starting line. The whole town was watching.

Luigi, the tyre store owner, was the starter. "On your marks, get set... GO!"

Lightning took off like a bullet leaving Doc sitting in his dust. After a few moments Doc slowly started down the track. It looked like there was no way he would ever catch Lightning. But just then, Lightning, who was heading into a turn, lost control and fell off a cliff landing in a cactus patch.

Doc caught up to him. "You drive like you fix roads... lousy."

After losing to Doc, Lightning went back to repairing the road. He worked all through the night, but this time he did the work properly. When the townsfolk woke the next morning they discovered a beautiful new patch of road. "E' bellisima! It's like it was paved by angels!"

As everyone enjoyed taking a spin on the new road, Lightning asked Sheriff to escort him to the dirt track. He wanted to get the turn he missed the day before. He tried again and again, but he kept skidding out.

Then Lightning realized Doc was watching. Doc tried to coach him. "If you're going hard enough left, you'll find yourself turning right."

But Lightning dismissed Doc's advice. What did he know about racing? "Crazy grandpa car."

The next morning Lightning was back at work on the road. All of the townsfolk were so inspired by how wonderful it looked that they began sprucing up their shops. The whole town was starting to look brand new. Sally stopped by and said Lightning could leave the impound and stay at the Cozy Cone Motel she owned.

That night Mater was in charge of watching Lightning. He took him out tractor tipping – a strange game where you sneak up on sleeping tractors and scare them with a loud noise. When the tractors woke up they were so startled that they would tip over. After sharing some laughs, they headed back to town.

As they drove, Mater teased Lightning. "You're in love with Miss Sally." As Mater continued teasing, he drove backwards. Lightning had never seen anything like it.

"Will you stop that! It's creeping me out. You're going to wreck or something."

"Wreck? Shoot, I'm the world's best backwards driver." Then, Mater put on an amazing display of backwards driving.

"Whoa! That was incredible! How'd you do that?"

"I'll teach you if you want?"

"Maybe I'll use it in my big race."

"What's so important about this race of yours anyway?"

"I've been dreaming about it my whole life. I'll be the first rookie in history ever to win it and when I do, we're talkin' big, new sponsor with private helicopters..."

"Hey you think maybe one day I could get a ride in one of them helicopters?

"Yeah, yeah, yeah, sure, sure."

Mater couldn't have been happier. "I knew it! I knowed I made a good choice."

"In what?"

"My best friend. See you tomorrow, buddy!"

The next day, as Lightning waited for Sheriff to give him his ration of gas, he peeked into Doc's garage. It was a mess. "Whoa Doc, time to clean out the garage buddy, come on." It was then that Lightning stumbled upon something unbelievable.

Just then, Doc entered. "Sign says 'Stay Out'."

"You have three Piston Cups. You're the 'Hudson Hornet'!"

Doc slammed the door in Lightning's face, but Lightning was so excited he raced to Flo's Cafe to tell everyone. But when he told them the news, no one believed him.

Then Sally invited Lightning to go for a drive. As they playfully raced up the mountain, Lightning was awed by the beautiful surroundings. When they got to the top Lightning turned to Sally. "How does a Porsche wind up in a place like this?"

"Well, it's really pretty simple. I was an attorney in L.A., living life in the fast lane."

"Oh, you were, were you?"

"And you know what? It never felt... happy."

"Yeah... I mean, really?"

"Yeah, so I left California – just drove and drove and finally broke down right here. Doc fixed me up. Flo took me in. Well, they all did. And I never left."

Lightning began to understand how much the town and its inhabitants meant to her. Finally, Sally shared her dream of returning Radiator Springs to its glory days. When they got back to town Lightning thanked her. "Thanks for the drive. I had a great time. It's kind of nice to slow down every once in a while."

A little while later, Lightning came upon Doc, racing alone out at the dirt track. He was truly impressed. When Doc realized he was being watched he left, but Lightning followed him back to his garage. "Doc, hold it, seriously, your driving's incredible!"

"Wonderful. Now go away."

"Hey, I mean it. You've still got it. Under the hood you and I are the same."

"We are not the same, understand? Now get out!" Doc went on to tell Lightning how the racing world had betrayed him long ago after he had a big crash.

"Doc, I'm not them."

"Oh, yeah? When is the last time you cared about something except yourself, hot rod? Just finish that road and get outta here!"

Early the next morning, the townsfolk awoke to find the road finished and no sign of Lightning. Flo expressed what they were all thinking. "He's gone?"

Just then Lightning appeared. Everyone was elated. "I knowed you wouldn't leave without saying goodbye."

"What are you doing here, son? You're gonna miss your race."

"But you know I can't go just yet."

Then Lightning said he needed new tyres from Luigi and Guido – which made them overjoyed. "Our first real customer in years!"

Next, Lightning got a case of Fillmore's organic fuel, some night vision goggles from Sarge, bumper stickers from Lizzie and a new paint job from Ramone. When his makeover was complete Sally couldn't believe her eyes. She knew what Lightning was doing. "Oh my goodness, looks like you've helped everybody in town."

Lightning even had a surprise for Sally. On his cue, the townsfolk turned on their newly repaired neon signs. Sally was amazed. The town was just like in its heyday. That night, the townsfolk cheerfully cruised under the new neon glow.

Suddenly, a hoard of vehicles swarmed into town. A helicopter hovered overhead. "We have found Lightning!" In an instant, the town was filled with reporters shouting and pushing. "Lightning! Will you still race for the Piston Cup?"

In the chaos, Mack pulled up and urged Lightning that it was time to go. He tried to say goodbye to Sally, but no words would come.

She spoke for him. "Thank you. Thanks for everything."

"Ah, it's just a road."

"No – it was much more than that. Good luck in California. I hope you find what you're looking for." Then she backed into the crowd and disappeared.

"Sally – Sally!"

As Mack pulled Lightning's trailer out of town, the swarm of reporters followed.

After things quieted down, Sally was shocked to learn that Doc had called the reporters to tell them where Lightning was. "It's best for everyone, Sally."

"Best for everyone, or best for you?"

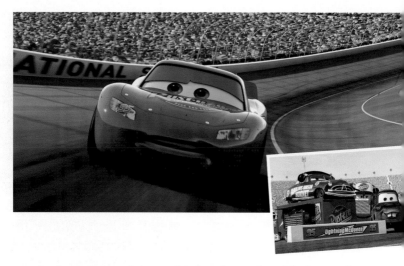

A few days later, Lightning should have been focused, but as he stood at the starting line of the big race all he could think of was Sally. He snapped out of his daydream to find the race had started without him.

As he tried to catch up to The King and Chick, Lightning started daydreaming again about Radiator Springs and his drive with Sally. When he snapped out of it he was heading straight for the wall! He hit his brakes hard and spun into the infield. Lightning was about to give up when a familiar voice came over his radio. "Hey, kid. You alright?"

"I don't know, Mack. I... I don't think I..."

"I didn't come all this way to see you quit." It was Doc! And when Lightning looked toward Pit Row, he saw all of his friends from Radiator Springs.

"Guys! You're here! I can't believe this!"

That's when Doc took over as his new crew chief. "Kid, get back out there."

Energized by his friends, Lightning pushed hard and was soon back into the race. He was more than a whole lap behind. The track announcer called the action. "Lightning passes them on the inside!"

"You're goin' great, kid. Just keep your head on."

On the next lap as Lightning tried to squeeze past, Chick bumped him, spinning him around backwards. But instead of falling behind, Lightning used Mater's backward driving technique and zoomed past him! Mater beamed. "I taught him that. Ka-chow."

"What a move by Lightning! He's caught up to the leaders!"

Chick was not about to come in behind Lightning. As he tried to overtake the rookie he bumped into him causing one of his tyres to blow. "Doc, I'm flat, I'm flat!" Lightning pulled into the pits where his friend Guido performed the fastest pit stop ever.

With new tyres on, Lightning roared back onto the track. After a few more laps, the white flag waved. It was the final lap. Doc encouraged him. "This is it, kiddo. You got four turns left."

The three cars screamed down the track. As Lightning tried to pass them on the inside, Chick bumped his rear end and sent him spinning towards the infield. But Lightning had one last trick up his sleeve. Using Doc's "turn right to go left" move, Lightning shot himself back onto the track and into the lead!

But as Lightning headed toward the chequered flag, he heard the crowd gasp. Chick had rammed into The King, knocking him out of the race. Up on the stadium screen, Lightning saw The King battered in the infield. It reminded him of Doc's big crash. Suddenly, instead of crossing the finish line, Lightning slammed on his brakes and went back to help the former champion.

The King was confused. "What are you doing, kid?"

"I think The King should finish his last race." Then, in an amazing display of good sportsmanship, Lightning pushed The King across the finish line. The crowd went wild, knowing that they were witnessing something very special. Because even though Lightning had finished in last place – he had shown everyone what a real champion was made of.

A few days later, Sally was at the top of the mountain admiring the view of Radiator Springs, when Lightning surprised her. "I hear this place is back on the map."

"It is?"

"Yeah, there's some rumour floating around that some hot shot, Piston Cup race car is setting up his big racing headquarters here."

"Really? Oh, well there goes the town." And with that, Sally raced off.

After a second, Lightning happily took off after her. "Yeah! Ka-chow!"

Well, that's the end of the road for this story, but if you ever find yourself driving across country, do yourself a favour and get off that big ol' Interstate and spend some time on the back roads. Who knows? With a little luck you just might come across a place as special as Radiator Springs.